Usborne Farmyard Tales

SCARECROW'S SECRET

Heather Amery

Illustrated by Stephen Cartwright

Language Consultant: Betty Root
Reading and Language Information Centre
University of Reading, England

There is a little yellow duck to find on every page.

This is Apple Tree Farm.

This is Mrs Boot, the farmer. She has two children, called Poppy and Sam, and a dog called Rusty.

Mr Boot is working in the barn.

"What are you doing, Dad?" asks Sam. "I'm
tying lots of straw on these poles," says Mr Boot.

"What is it?"

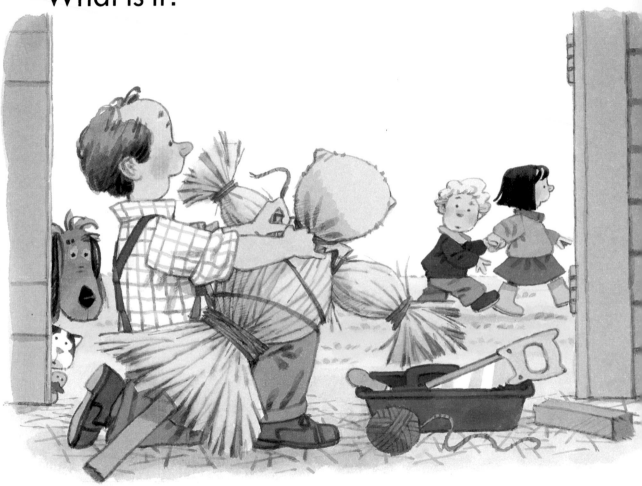

"You'll soon see," says Dad. "Go and get my old coat from the shed, please. Bring my old hat too."

4

"It's going to be a scarecrow."

Poppy and Sam come back with the coat and hat.
Then they help Mr Boot put them on the scarecrow.

"He's just like a nice old man."

"I've got some old gloves for him," says Sam.
"Let's call him Mr Straw," says Poppy.

"He's finished now."

"Help me carry him, please, Poppy," says Mr
Boot. "You bring the spade, Sam."

They all go to the corn field.

Mr Boot digs a hole in the field. Then he pushes
the pole in so that Mr Straw stands up.
8

"He does look real."

"I'm sure Mr Straw will scare off all the birds,"
says Sam. "Especially the crows," says Poppy.

Mr Straw is doing a good job.

Every day Mr Boot, Poppy and Sam look at Mr
Straw. There are no birds in the corn field.

"There's Farmer Dray's scarecrow."

"He's no good at all," says Sam. "The birds are eating all the corn and standing on the scarecrow."

"Why is Mr Straw so good?"

"Sometimes he looks as if he is moving," says Poppy. "His coat goes up and down. It's very odd."

"Let's go and look."

"Let's creep up very quietly," says Sam. And they
tiptoe across the corn field to look at Mr Straw.

"There's something inside his coat."

"It's moving about," says Poppy. "And it's making a funny noise. What is it?" says Sam.

14

"It's our cat and her kittens."

Carefully they open the coat. There is Whiskers,
the cat, and two baby kittens hiding in the straw.

"So that's scarecrow's secret."

"Whiskers is helping Mr Straw to frighten off the birds," says Poppy. "Clever Mr Straw," says Sam.

First published in 1990 by Usborne Publishing Ltd, Usborne House, 83-85 Saffron Hill, London EC1N 8RT, England. Copyright © 1990 Usborne Publishing Ltd.

The name Usborne and the device ⬮ are Trade Marks of Usborne Publishing Ltd. All rights reserved. No part of this publication may be reproduced, stored in a retrieval system or transmitted by any form or by any means, electronic, mechanical, photocopy, recording or otherwise, without the prior permission of the publisher.
Printed in Portugal.